Tobias, the Quig and the Rumplenut Tree

Written and illustrated by Tim Robinson

Winslow Press
Delray Beach, Florida • New York

Tobias, the quig, and the rumplenut tree,
this is their story, the story of three,
the story of three who depended upon
one another forever, forever and on . . .

The Quig

The quig was a bird with fabulous plumes,
the kind kept by people, in cages, in rooms,
for the pleasure of those who might never have seen
a quig in the wild where he'd rather have been.

Now, the quig was enthroned in a glorious cage,
gilded and gleaming, at just center stage,
in a parlor surrounded by treasures procured
from mysterious places his owners had toured.
They brought something back from wherever they went,
to make sure that the fabulous quig was content.

And yes, he was grateful for being adored,
but something outside just could not be ignored.
For beyond a large window and up on a rise
grew a rumplenut tree right in front of his eyes.
Now, a rumplenut tree to a quig is a home
(in the wild where they live in a group, not alone)
with its branches all twisted, around and around,
and rumplenuts spread out all over the ground.
This beacon, this vision from where he was born,
put the quig in a quandary, divided and torn.
He knew as a pet this is where he should be,
But his heart and his soul both longed to be free.

And so the quig dreamed
of the rumplenut tree.

The Rumplenut Tree

Now the rumplenut tree was himself in a rut.
The trees that were once by his side had been cut.
On the rise he stood sadly, all but alone,
except for some stumps and a wall made of stone.
Solitude, though, was just half of the thing.
See, the rumplenut tree needed someone with wings,
someone with wings and the instinct to know
just where a rumplenut's likely to grow.
For right now the rumplenuts fell in the shade,
the shade that the rumplenut foliage made,
ample and lush, so green and verdured,
so thick that the light from the sun was obscured.

In the wild, on the island where rumplenuts grow,
quigs do the work of a farmer. They sow.
They carry the nuts in their beaks from the shade
to the places where young trees from old nuts are made.
But here on the rise there were no quigs at all
to carry the nuts from the shade past the wall.
It seemed a solution might never be found,
and new trees might never break through the ground.
It needed the quig, and the quig wanted out,
and they each needed someone to bring it about.

And so to Tobias to figure it out.

Tobias

Tobias, being the gardener's boy,
preferred things with leaves to playing with toys—
flowers and shrubberies, cabbage and peas,
but mostly Tobias liked climbing in trees.

Sycamores, birches, alders, and elms,
he saw them as ships with himself at their helms.
He imagined spectacular, glorious feats,
commanding a vast and notorious fleet.
The pride of them all, the most noble to see,
was the ship that he saw in the rumplenut tree.
He'd climb on its branches and shelter his eyes
to scan the horizon for pirates and spies.
He would look to the left and then to the right,
steer close to the wind and outrun the night.

On one such excursion he spotted a bird
who stared from a cage toward a place it preferred.
He followed its eyes to the rumplenut tree,
and he knew then and there what his mission would be.
He must free this bird, this glorious thing.
He would open its cage and let it take wing...
but the window was high, and Tobias was small.
He wasn't too sure he could reach it at all.

And so to the plan and the stilts and the fall.

Tobias recalled somewhere deep in the shed,
way out in back of the vegetable bed,
were some long scraps of wood, a hammer and nails—
so he tossed out the anchor and quick luffed the sails.
He jumped from the tree, and after two tries,
he vaulted the wall and ran down the rise.
He sprinted the property, charged through the shed
and set to the purpose alive in his head.
After some clanging and banging around,
he emerged from the shed two more feet off the ground.
Tall enough now on the stilts he had made,
Tobias set out to accomplish his raid.

SQUASH
TOMATO
NAILS

He stilted his way to the window that faced
the rumplenut tree, and he carefully placed
his face to the glass to size up the task
and to ask the one question he needed to ask.
"Do you want to be free?" he queried the bird,
and the quig nodded "Yes," so he knew it had heard.

With one hand Tobias then threw wide the panes
and opened the cage with the hand that remained.
His stilts fell away and he fell to the ground
with a crash and a bang and a terrible sound.

And so the quig's freedom and what
it brought 'round.

The quig stretched his wings and shot through the air,
from his old home, the cage, to the tree over there.
He was long out of practice and stiffened by years.
The joy flooded up from his heart through his tears.
Life among branches was as it should be.
He feasted his eyes on the bounteous tree—
leafy green ceilings with rumplenut walls,
with rumplenuts lining long rumplenut halls.
Instinct took over (that happens with birds).
No order, no question, no lesson, no words.

One by one, in his beak, he gathered up nuts
and did what he knew he should do in his guts.
He would eat one for strength, then with purposeful eyes,
he would fly one nut out, past the wall, down the rise.

The quig knew inside how to sow, as I've said,
like a farmer at dawn when he rolls out of bed.
In rows, up and down, in the field past the wall,
he planted 'til dawn, then he let out a call . . .
a call for assistance, one urgent and true,
and somehow Tobias knew just what to do.
The quig's work completed, new work had begun:
Tend to the nuts 'til they sprout toward the sun.

And so grew an orchard from where there was none.

The years turned like pages, Tobias grew tall.
So did the trees, but the quig, he stayed small.
Together they prospered, the bird and the man.
And the trees that from nuts had grown up from the land.
Then slowly, in numbers, more quigs found their way
from gold cages elsewhere, from lives colored gray.
Quigs nested, quigs hatched, so many, so new.
Tobias got married and raised children, too.
They now climb those trees as Tobias had done—
imagining galleons inside every one.

And so stories pass from the old to the young.